TAD and DAD

words and pictures by
David Ezra Stein

SCHOLASTIC INC.

This is for Sam,

for all our daytimes and nighttimes together.

And to all the dads who are sleeping on the couch tonight.

ISBN 978-1-338-05349-4

Copyright © 2015 by David Ezra Stein. All rights reserved. Published by Scholastic Inc.,
557 Broadway, New York, NY 10012, by arrangement with Nancy Paulsen Books,
an imprint of Penguin Young Readers Group, a division of Penguin Random House LLC.
SCHOLASTIC and associated logos are trademarks and/or registered trademarks of Scholastic Inc.

12 11 10 9 8 7 6 5 4 3   19 20 21

Printed in the U.S.A.   40

First Scholastic printing, April 2016

Design by Ryan Thomann
Text set in Handy Sans
To make the final art for this book, the artist first copied Crayola-marker line drawings
onto watercolor paper. Watercolor was added using a single large, round brush,
building up many layers of transparent color. Care was taken to
encourage and preserve happy accidents. Crayon was added as an accent.

My dad has big, buggy eyes, strong legs, and a huge mouth.

He sings in a loud

BUUURRPP

that echoes across the pond.

And I love him.

As soon as I could wiggle,
I swam everywhere with my dad.

Dad tried to tuck me in at night, but—

SPLASH!

I followed him
to **his** bed.

I went to sleep and dreamt
that I could swim as fast as Dad.

And then,
I grew legs.

That day,
I reached new heights.

Dad tried
to tuck me in
at night, but—

SPLASH!

I followed him to his bed.

That night, I dreamt I was
the best jumper in the world, like Dad.

And then

I grew a big mouth,
and I could sing.

Good morning, Dad!

That day, the pond was alive
with the sound of music,
made by me and Dad.

Dad tried to tuck me in at night, but—

SPLASH!

"It's me, Tad!" I said.

That night I dreamt
I could sing as loud as Dad.

And then
I grew really big,
and I was very hungry.

That day, we helped ourselves to a feast.

Look at me, Dad!

"Tad!" said Dad. "When you jump in my bed, I can't sleep because you're always wiggling and poking, kicking and croaking!"

"I didn't know that," I said.

"Why do you want to sleep in my bed?" said Dad.

"Are you trying to drive me **bananas?**"

"I'm sorry, Dad. But don't worry, I don't want to sleep in your bed anymore, anyway . . . **you snore!**"

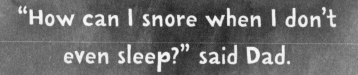

"How can I snore when I don't
even sleep?" said Dad.

"Goodnight, Dad," I said.

For the first time,
I swam away from Dad.

"Ahhh," said Dad.
"Peace at last."

I tried to go to sleep,
but I heard a big hubbub.

Someone huge
was splashing around.

FRoG-GONE-IT! said a loud voice.

I couldn't believe my eyes.
It was Dad.
He was wiggling and poking,
kicking and croaking.
He was splashing around
and making a big ruckus.

"I think I know
what you need, Dad—
a little company," I said.

"Is that
better, Dad?"

"Maybe better . . ."
he said.

Soon Dad was fast asleep.

zZzZ^z

I was right!
I knew he would miss me!